Fruit Rot

James R. Gapinski

Etchings Press
Indianapolis, Indiana

This publication is made possible by your donations to the Friends of Etchings Press with additional support from the Shaheen College of Arts and Sciences and the Department of English at the University of Indianapolis. Special thanks to the students who judged, edited, designed, and published this chapbook: Hope Coleman, Carrie Long, and Erin Taylor.

UNIVERSITY *of*
INDIANAPOLIS®

Published by Etchings Press
1400 E. Hanna Ave.
Indianapolis, Indiana 46227
All rights reserved

etchings.uindy.edu
www.uindy.edu/cas/english

Printed by IngramSpark

Published in the United States of America

ISBN 978-1-0878-9821-6
24 23 22 21 20   1 2 3 4 5

Colophon:
The book interior is set with LTC Caslon
The cover is set in TW Cen MT and LTC Caslon

Cover image by Couleur via Pixabay
Cover design by Hope Coleman
Interior design by Hope Coleman

Fruit Rot

James R. Gapinski

Fruit Rot

Lacey and I need money. She's depressed again, and we can't afford therapy. I've been working nights at a convenience store, and she sells tchotchke crap on Etsy—which only makes matters worse, because she'd rather be crafting something worthwhile or working on a new painting. On a daily basis, she asks "Why do shitty fridge magnets sell, but nobody buys anything *real* online?" Then she mumbles a lot and skips dinner. She puts up a pissed-off front, but underneath she's just sad. I think that's sort of what Frank Castle is actually like, hiding behind that macho *Punisher* stuff. Lacey takes St. John's Wort from Walgreens. The bottle touts a natural remedy for "mood improvement." It doesn't work. She says she needs real drugs, but that takes real money.

I storyboard my new superhero comic. It's about a guy who discovers Old McDonald's secret GMO lab, and then he mutates into a super strong half-pig hybrid thing and uses his power to fight for food justice. I'm going for some kind of subtle satire, but Lacey says it's not subtle at all. Her exact words are "That's so fucking obvious. And Old McDonald? Like from the nursery rhyme? Really?"

I prepare a pitch anyway. The rep for Image tells me "Nobody wants new heroes. If you ain't doing existing DC or Marvel IP, then forget it. Superheroes are played out. Write something real, or try Dynamite." The Dynamite guy just says "No" without much explanation.

I try to write something real. I write about Lacey and how she was beaten by her father. But by page three she already discovers that she's part of a secret society that protects humanity from aliens. Her dad becomes an alien on page ten, and she kills him on page twelve. I toss the draft after page sixteen, wherein Lacey's newly upgraded robotic arm malfunctions. What the fuck is wrong with me?

I show the storyboards to Lacey, and she says "Of course it sucks. You don't even know the whole story with my dad. And it's not like you can write vicariously through my past traumas."

"But what about the alien part? That was kind of cool, right?"

She doesn't respond, but her look is answer enough.

I need some fresh air and a fresh perspective. I limp out of the spare bedroom, shuffle around the hole in our stairs, and sit on the porch. I prop my messed-up leg on the nearby footstool and lean back. I want to do some pensive skyline staring, like in the movies, but there's a tree blocking my view. There wasn't a tree yesterday. Not even a bud. Our front yard has always been a barren dirt patch.

This mystery tree is huge, and the bark is a perfect Silver Age green, like it jumped right off the *Incredible Hulk #2* cover. The tree has sparkly leaves and golden fruit sprouting from its nuclear green arms. The fruit is round like an orange, but shiny like a ripe apple.

"Lacey, there's a tree in our yard," I say.

"No there isn't," Lacey yells from inside.

"Yes there is," I say. I pluck a golden fruit from the tree as proof. I drop it on Lacey's desk.

She looks up from her hot glue gun. "Oh, I see," she says.

"Can we eat it?" I ask.

"That's your first thought? Eating it?"

"It could help reduce our food bills," I say. "Maybe we can use the savings to patch the hole in the stairs."

"The savings? I don't think annual our fruit budget is all that big," she says.

I take a bite. It tastes like Pixy Stix.

I offer Lacey a taste, but before she bites it, the fruit turns blackish, and small bugs crawl from its dark flesh. Lacey shrieks and throws the fruit. It splats against the floor, oozing black guts and sending a cadre of bugs scurrying into the floorboards. "What the hell! It's rotten," she screams.

"It tasted fine to me. I'll get something to clean it up," I say. I take a step toward the kitchen, and my knee doesn't buckle. I take a second step; the joint is smooth. I grab a dishtowel and sprint back across the house. My messed-up leg feels brand new. In fact, my entire body seems fine-tuned. There are none of the usual aches and throbs that accompany the movements of a thirty-year-old man with no health insurance, no exercise regimen, and a food stamp diet.

Lacey and I pluck some more fruit that evening and try to bake a pie. Within a few seconds of slicing into the fruit, its flesh turns black and spews bugs again. I spend the rest of the night hunting and smashing bugs with my shoe. I'm actually glad for the opportunity to chase the insects; it lets me show off my newly rediscovered fine-motor skills, sharp reflexes, and limp-free leg. I can't decide if I feel like Superman after he soaks up rejuvenating sunbeams or Batman when he gets that kickass super-suit circa Frank Miller's magnum opus. Probably Superman, since Batman was getting mechanical assistance—but in truth, I'd rather be Batman.

I begin redrafting my Old McDonald character. He turns into Ronald McDonald. I try to make him more devious and scary, and he becomes something like a hillbilly farmer crossed with the Joker. The concept sketch doesn't make any sense, but I like the weird image of Joker with a pitchfork, so I put it on the fridge using one of Lacey's Etsy magnets.

Next week, Lacey gets the flu. On a hunch, I ask her to eat the fruit.

"What if it gets gross again?" she asks.

"It seems okay," I tell her. "I think it only gets rotten after it's cut open."

She gives me a strange glance while taking a quick bite and a slow swallow. The remaining portion of fruit turns black and buggy in her hand. I hold up a small trashcan, but Lacey misses the can and the black goop slides down the wall.

"How do you feel?" I ask.

"Good," she says. She sounds hesitant, like she doesn't believe the transformation. She takes her temperature. It's normal. She takes it again. Normal. Again. Normal. She goes to the bathroom mirror and inspects her nasal passages. She tries to blow her nose and nothing comes out. She takes her temperature again. I leave her to her inspections.

After an hour, she comes downstairs. "Babe, I'm one-hundred-percent better," she says with more confidence.

"I know," I say.

"No, listen to me. One-hundred-percent. Not just the flu. My hysterectomy scars are gone. That kink in my neck is gone. Everything. I feel new."

I drain my pitiful bank account and put an ad in the paper. Lacey says "Nobody reads the paper," and she puts an ad on Craigslist instead. Twelve people show up for our miracle fruit. Eleven respond from Craigslist—they are sick and need cures. One responds from the newspaper ad—he is a lawyer. The lawyer hands us some watermarked forms about a possible lawsuit for false advertising, FDA noncompliance, and some violation for bringing an invasive species into the neighborhood. He puts away the eco-violation after woman's goiter shrinks. He pockets the FDA paperwork when an ex-boxer's cauliflower-ear reforms into its original shape. And he ditches the false advertising claim when a gaunt, cancer-ridden woman regains pigment, regrows hair, and rises from her wheelchair. By the time all eleven people are cured, the lawyer wants to buy a piece of fruit for some unseen ailment. Lacey tells him it'll be double. He grumbles and obliges.

The next day, word of mouth delivers us dozens of new clients. Lacey tries to explain supply and demand to me while painting over yesterday's prices with much, much higher rates. I don't get it, but I trust her. A few years ago, Lacey took some business courses, back when she had dreams of opening her own gallery.

We sell even more fruit than the day before, despite the higher prices. I decide it's best to let Lacey handle all business-related fruit issues. She knows what she's doing. She hires the nosy lawyer, forms an LLC, and gets our house rezoned for agricultural production and sale. Meanwhile, I use some of the profits to fix the hole in our stairs—now that my leg is healed, I don't want it getting fucked up again.

When Lacey finishes staffing and zoning, the front yard reopens to a line that stretches past the horizon. Our fruit tree attracts sickly people, movie stars, news crews, research scientists who want to synthesize this miracle cure, and self-proclaimed millionaires who say money is no object. Lacey raises the price several more times. She teaches me how to use spreadsheets, and we track the progress of our exponential bank account. In less than a month, we go from Peter Parker dirt-shit poor to Bruce Wayne mega wealthy.

But we soon face a new problem. The huge demand, falling supply, and sky-high prices breed desperate sob stories. People take off their clothes and show us their sickly bodies in hopes of pity. Mothers and fathers spin sob stories about dying children. Pity. Guilt. Sorrow. We want to help everybody, but there are fewer and fewer available fruits each day. I track it all on my fancy spreadsheets. I show Lacey the numbers, she applauds my newfound business acumen, and we both decide that we need to carefully manage our remaining supply.

We erect fences around our property to protect ourselves from the mob. We interview security guards and hire them on long-term contracts. It feels like a cross between a regular business and a prison, complete with searchlights and razor-wire.

With the perimeter secure, we chart a more reasonable plan for daily sales. I take inventory of the remaining fruit globes. I prepare a brief report for Lacey—she is, after all, the CFO, CEO, and President of our LLC. Basically, the report recommends that we only sell one fruit per day. At that rate, the supply will last us for a couple months—with estimated golden fruit market growth rates, those couple months will net enough income for us to live comfortably for our entire lives.

We post a sign saying *One customer per day*, and the crowd screams. The guards form a barrier, brandish clubs, and order is restored. Some people cry, and I need to look away. I remind myself that the money from our sales will help Lacey and me. She'll no longer burn herself with a glue gun and use it as an excuse to let out a week's worth of sobs. And maybe after some more therapy sessions, she'll know what's making her sad, and we can work on it together. Then we can get married, and maybe we'll get a cat named Selina—after Catwoman, of course.

We make a single sale to somebody claiming to work for Apple; he says the fruit can bring Steve Jobs back to life, but I don't think the fruit works that way. He signs the waiver, and the lawyer stamps a seal of approval, so it's no longer our problem. After the two-minute transaction, we close shop and the guards shoot beanbag bullets at the crowd in controlled bursts followed by a teargas finale.

I lock the gate and spend time on a new comic. I sit underneath the fruit tree, and I write stories about similarly strange trees with mysterious origins, and this gives way to a character who can control trees. And soon enough there are vines and flowers and a whole family of plants. The character loves the plants and treats them like his own children. In turn, they love him, and they obey his commands. At first I think it's artsy and that I'm doing a magical realist story rather than a superhero motif. But when I show five splash pages to Lacey, she says "So it's a superhero with plant powers or something? I guess that's kind of cool. A little different from having animal powers."

"No, it's not a superhero story," I say.

"Yeah, it is."

I look at the sketch again. I realize she's right. I've created a good-guy version of something like Poison Ivy. I think my character is dissimilar enough that I won't get sued by DC, but I ask the lawyer anyway. He says it's not his area of expertise, but he thinks I'm safe. I draw some

9

more vines and globes of golden fruit dangling underneath the character's arms, and I decide that I like the concept. I want to work on this project. It feels right. So what if superheroes are played out? Lacey and I pull a huge fruit-seller salary now, and I can afford to self-publish. I can do it right. I can bring back the Golden Age of comics, with its drama, heroics, and out-of-this-world stories. All I need is a villain. You can't have Batman without Joker. Spiderman needs Doctor Octopus. Superman needs Lex Luthor.

At first I use the sketch of Lacey's dad again—in extraterrestrial form, of course. I think that maybe the aliens want to invade, but they breathe carbon dioxide, so they are killing off the earth's plants to deplete the atmospheric oxygen, sort of like terraforming. And maybe the plant-hero-guy protects the forest and fights the aliens. It sounds stupider the more I outline the plot. It'll never do.

I draw another sketch of farmer Joker trying to inject pesticides into the superhero's plant children. Lacey walks by and laughs. It isn't supposed to be funny. I crumple the drawing and get ready for bed.

The next day, the first person in line cannot afford our price. Neither can the second. Or the third. We hear sob story after sob story as we work through the window-shoppers. About twenty or thirty people into the line, somebody finally ponies up the dough—a woman with a bandaged arm, a leg that bends the wrong way, and a burn on one half of her face. She reminds me of Two Face, and I think about knockoff versions that might work with my story—a plant that's dipped in acid, or maybe a greedy CEO who flips coins to decide which rainforests to destroy.

The crowd tries to push through. The guards conk a few heads with nightsticks, and that seems to be the end of it. The woman wipes off the fruit. "Just in case you use pesticides," she says.

"We don't," I say.

"Can't ever be too careful."

She takes a bite of the golden prize. Her arm makes popping noises as it reassembles itself beneath the bandages. Her leg and foot do a one-eighty, and her red face becomes soft and flesh-toned again. Most of the crowd and the guards are awestruck at the instant healing process—they've seen others eat the fruit, but most illnesses are less visible. Taking advantage of the distraction, a scrawny guy bolts through the crowd and grabs the woman's fruit. The guards swing their batons, but they can't connect with the agile man. He does a tuck-and-roll maneuver, skidding to a stop near the base of the tree. He holds up the stolen, half-eaten fruit. It blackens and bugs coat his hands. He closes his eyes and bites it anyway. Nothing happens. "What the fuck?" he says, rotten, tar-like juice drips from his mouth. The guards smack his kneecaps, and he goes down. The guards pummel him; he loses a tooth and his fingers bend backwards.

The news media is always lingering around our property, and they interview the fruit thief immediately after the guards redeposit him amongst the ever-growing line.

I release a statement: "He was trespassing on private property, he stole company property, and we had every right to forcibly recover aforementioned property." News teams document his injuries. We get phone calls within five minutes. A helicopter is overhead in ten. I release another statement, offering to pay his medical bills in a show of good faith—I don't even notice the funds leaving our bank account, these thousands of dollars are meaningless now. The goodwill gesture pacifies people until the evening news. A camera crew visits the guy's home; they discover his family turned to blackish, shriveled corpses. They visit the scrawny guy in the hospital. There's a close-up on the scrawny guy's agony as he watches the footage of his dead family.

The lawyer recommends we do some testing. Without accurate data, he can't address the liability factors. I know I should be more horrified, more empathetic, more anything other than defensive—but somehow, all I can think to do is protect the business. The business *does* help people, after all. Our once-daily customer is cured. It's a miracle. Lacey and I provide miracles. And we're finally living our own lives. We're happy. I didn't used to be happy, and there's something about being happy that makes you less inclined to care about the shittiness of everybody else's lives.

We hire a scientist for a ridiculous sum of money—this time, I notice the difference at the ATM. The scientist performs tests on mice from PetSmart. She breeds the mice—it doesn't take long; mice have sex like crazy, and they give birth quickly. She has entire family units in different cages. She feeds a mouse some rotten fruit. It has no effect on the mouse who ingests it, but the entire immediate family shrivels and dies in a rush of black blood and grotesque mousy shrieks and chirps. She repeats the test a dozen times. The results are always the same: ingesting rotten fruit kills off the entire immediate family.

I sit in front of the few mice still alive in the lab. I write about a new villain and attempt a sketch. He is an evil scientist who breeds super mice that infect people with some mystery illness. The infected people have black blood, and they commit atrocious murders. Eventually, almost every human on earth falls ill, and the plant-hero-guy worries it'll spread to trees next. So he develops a robot army to fight the murderous, infected masses. The robots rip open the diseased corpses and drink the black blood for fuel, and I realize I've drawn General Blackblood from *2000AD*, so I backtrack. In my new version, the diseased mice bite the scientist, and she turns into a rodent. My preliminary sketches look like Splinter from *TNMT*. Why the fuck is it so hard to come up with an original villain? Hell, I don't even care if it's original—it can be another rip-off—I just want it to feel natural. I want the hero/villain struggle to be embedded into every aspect of the story. I want the reader to know the stakes from page one, and I want to recapture that epic struggle of good versus evil. I need a grotesque, bad-to-the-bone Venom, not some complicated Harry Osborn shit.

None of it's working. I crumple the pages and relay the scientist's findings to Lacey and the lawyer.

"Shit," Lacey says. She pokes a dead mouse with a pencil.

"Yeah, I know. It sucks. I don't want this to happen again. We need more security," I say.

"No, you need more lawyers," the lawyer says.

We hire both. We also add high-tech cameras, motion sensors, knockout gas, and snares.

Even though the lawyer says we could've won the suit, Lacey and I decide it's best to settle with the scrawny guy out of court. The lawyer and his new legal team update the waiver and assure that our liability is zero again.

The line still stretches past the horizon, despite the bad press. Lacey is hesitant to reopen, but we have to sell some fruit, otherwise we'll run dry eventually—all the security and legal fees are pricey, and Lacey has appointments to see an expensive celebrity therapist twice a week now.

After the grand reopening, things go smoothly for about a week.

The next security breach is better planned than the scrawny guy's mad dash. As a wealthy man exits with his expensive fruit in a locked icebox, a woman slips past the gate before it clanks shut. She's got a gas mask, and she is unphased by the chemical mist enveloping her small frame. Her Kevlar vest repels beanbag rounds, but all this heavy equipment doesn't help her outmaneuver the ring of guards. They tackle her. I warn them not to beat her too badly—we don't want more negative press. She puts up a fight, but they eventually toss her outside.

We close shop and map out some new security measures. As the blueprints grow, we discover that we've outlined plans for a fortress, and even the once-daily customer will have a tough time getting in. I put down my pencil and suggest a different approach: "What if we stop letting anybody inside?"

"What do you mean?" Lacey asks.

"Look at the security we already have. It's crazy.

But people are still finding a way inside. Let's get rid of the line altogether. Get rid of the risk. Buy out the neighborhood. Give the guards permission to incapacitate anybody setting foot on the exterior properties. Have some peace and quiet again."

"How will that work? I mean, we do have a chunk of change saved, but what about keeping the business going? We have expenses now. We need to keep selling."

"Let's set up a foundation. We can have the foundation read through all the requests for fruit and make some autonomous decisions. Take us out of the loop. Ship everything off-site. Keep it in some vault somewhere. No more of this daily stuff. Release one or two pieces of fruit per-year. Keep prices really high. Let the lawyer sort it out. He's good at that logistical stuff."

"I guess that could work," Lacey says. "So, basically, we'd be retiring?"

I shrug. "Sort of. We'd still collect checks."

We pluck most of the fruit, leaving a few dangling near the top of the tree—our private reserve. We vacuum pack the fruit and hand it off to the lawyer, a security team, and the foundation's newly appointed president. We watch our stress-level fall and our bank account rise once more. We keep seeing more zeros at the end of each statement, even as we make gigantic withdraws to buy out and fortify the entire neighborhood.

Along with more security, we decide to make other improvements. We use a fraction of a percent of our newfound wealth to convert the house next-door into a full-service spa. We let the guards use it every now and then, but it's mostly for us. We turn another nearby house into a basketball court—this is mainly so I can continue to show off my limp-free leg to nobody in particular.

Next, we renovate our house. We get new appliances, hardwood floors, granite countertops, new insulation, new plumbing, new wiring. The works. The entire place looks shiny and perfect.

We designate the attic and basement for our personal whims. Lacey converts the attic into an artist's loft, and she celebrates by purchasing a fifty-foot canvas, super expensive zebra-hair paintbrushes, and seven crates of assorted paints. She burns her Etsy tchotchkes beneath the tree with its sparkling leaves and golden fruit, and she dances in the shimmering reflections and roaring flames. In a display of unfettered joy, she leaps through the fire and burns her ankles—but she eats a piece of fruit and restores her legs to their original state. Meanwhile, I convert the basement into a Batcave replica; I buy an authentic Batsuit signed by Michael Keaton; I wire all our new surveillance equipment to LCD screens in the Batcave. It's like the real deal.

I spend most nights in the basement Batcave while Lacey paints in the attic studio. We consistently meet back up at midnight to rediscover the sexual spark we had years ago.

For a while, I keep the Batsuit in a glass display case, not wanting to risk tainting its pristine condition. But eventually my impulse control breaks down, and I wear the thing around the Batcave. I draw some new villains, but they all turn into some variant of Joker fused with some other Batman character. The Joker and Robin hybrid is by far the most amusing new sketch, but it doesn't get me closer to a usable villain—and it's still not as good as my original Joker farmer sketch.

I try to reboot my brainstorming session with a sketch of Lacey, but she turns out looking like Harley Quinn. I'm about to try again when the Batcave lights up. Warning LEDs flicker and three cameras go dark. I run outside. A woman sits atop the razor-wire wearing a thick burlap bodysuit designed to keep the wire from flaying her skin. She sprays black paint on a fourth camera. She hops to the ground and reminds me of a burlap-clad Catwoman. The guards pelt her with beanbags. She doesn't go down.

The woman bolts toward the fruit. Some snares encircling the tree snap to life, and she writhes on the ground. The guards ziptie her hands while I remove the snares. One guard shines a Maglite on her face. It's the same woman from months earlier—the one who outwitted the knockout gas countermeasures. "Stay off our property," I say.

"I just want one," she says.

"So does everybody else. It wouldn't be fair to give you one while everybody else pleads their case and waits their turn. Submit your request to the foundation," I say.

"No, you don't understand," she says.

"Yes, I do," I say, and I decide I've had enough. I gesture for the guards to take her away. I go back inside. I sit down, and the Batsuit's cape bunches up beneath my ass. I wriggle around and shove the cape aside. It's only then that I realize I was dressed as a superhero while I told a pleading woman that I couldn't help her. I pull off the black mask and throw it into the glass display case. "Fuck!" I scream out loud. I never wanted any of this. I decide that maybe I need therapy too. I go upstairs to ask Lacey about it—I've never been to therapy before, and it sounds kind of iffy. She holds up a pregnancy test strip with two lines on it. "I guess the fruit healed my uterus too."

"What? How? It was gone. Removed completely," I grab the test strip and shake it, thinking maybe that'll fix the error. Double lines.

"Yeah, well, we've seen the fruit grow back missing flesh and bone on other people, right? Why not internal organs too?"

I try to draw some more villains while we wait for the doctor. Lacey tells me to stop, and she grabs the pencil and pad. The ultrasound confirms a tiny embryo. The doctor points out various features. The head, the body, a circle that the doctor says is the yolk sac—I didn't know human embryos had yolks. I place my arm around Lacey's shoulders. She asks the doctor about her recently prescribed antidepressants and if she should stop taking them. She asks about sex and if we can still have it. She asks about the sauna and if that's somehow bad for the baby. She asks and she asks, and her hand moves across my sketchpad. I assume she's writing down the doctor's answers, but when she hands it back to me, I see there are baby names scrawled on the first page. The second page contains a swooping curvilinear sketch of what might've been an obtuse ultrasound. It's a beautiful drawing, like the ones Lacey used to do when galleries were still interested in her work, before Etsy and before hysterectomies. Her artwork had always been described as motherly. I'm not sure that my comics could ever be called fatherly.

Lacey puts a copy of the ultrasound on our fridge, next to my farmer Joker sketch. She also frames two copies: one for her attic and one for my Batcave. I take the ultrasound out of the frame and pocket it. In the empty frame, I place Lacey's sketch. The sketch is our child—I can see our baby in the sketch, clearer than the fuzzy blob of an ultrasound.

I go through storage boxes until I find Lacey's old grad-school work. I see the same ovals and lines and arcs. I see babies and mothers and fathers and Lacey and me. But mostly, I see love. And I understand why Lacey is happy when she paints, and why Etsy had been killing her, and why my failed comics feel like personal deficiencies. I need to create a villain, and soon. I need to write this story before our child is born. It's our story, and it needs a happy ending. A superhero story can't end happily unless the villain is defeated.

I think about cube-like villains to fight the plant-hero-guy and his curvilinear embryonic sidekick. I draw old-school cubist robots, like Alice from the *Jetsons*. The drawings suck, but I keep sketching, knowing that eventually my lines will form something usable. A loud bang startles me, and my pencil splinters in half. I pull a piece of graphite out of my pinky. It's too dark outside for most of the cameras to pick up anything, but the motion sensors are clean, so it's probably nothing. Still, I feel like I should investigate. This time, I actually remember to take off the Batsuit first.

I trip over an incapacitated guard, and my knee twists. With my reacquired limp, I hobble to the breaker and hit the floodlights. Another incapacitated guard is next to the tree, directly across from a heap of deactivated snares. Another guard is bleeding out while yet another guard cradles his head. "I panicked when I saw the bodies. I switched to live rounds and started shooting. I thought he was the intruder," the guard shouts.

I brush my hands through the dense, sparkling leaves, hoping to find a piece of fruit to save this dying man. There are none within reach. "I need to get the ladder," I say.

"His pulse is dropping fast," the guard tells me. I start to limp away when a woman jumps down from the tree holding a golden fruit in her hand. She's got Kevlar again and some sort of high-tech goggles. Her belt could be mistaken for a fully functional Batbelt with its zippered pouches, several ropes, two grappling hooks, stun gun, chloroform bottle, compass, and some electronic doodad that I don't recognize.

The high-tech, ninja-like intruder lifts her goggles. I recognize her from earlier—the increasingly wily repeat offender. "I'm sorry. I didn't want your guards to get hurt," she says. She extends her hand. The guard flinches before realizing that she's offering the golden fruit. He tries to bite it, but he's too weak. His skin loses pigment and his eyes droop, his chapped lips still wrapped around the fruit's unbroken skin. The other guard helps move the jawbone, forcing a big bite. I massage the dying man's throat while the woman crouches next to me, pressing her hands on the guard's gunshot wound. Blood bubbles through her fingers. The guard swallows and makes some hoarse noises. The blood stops, and the intruder lifts her fingers. The guard's flesh is pink and new. He opens his eyes. He'll live, thanks to the fruit.

The intruder wipes away the leftover blood and grabs the blackened fruit from the guard's hand. "Thank you," he says.

She begins to walk away, and I call out "Wait, you can't eat the black ones. Please, let me get you a fresh golden one. You deserve it."

"No I don't," she says.

"Yeah you do. You could've just ran off and let him die. You could've gotten away with it. Instead, you gave him the fruit."

"But I don't need a fresh one," she says.

"No, listen," I say. "The rotten ones will kill your whole family."

"I know," she says. She walks toward the fence. I limp beside her.

"You know?"

"Yes. I want the black one. That's all I ever wanted."

She climbs the fence and wriggles through a section of clipped razor-wire. The backup team arrives and encircles her escape route through the alley. She drops from the fence and looks at me through the chain-link. The guards inch closer, but I hold up my hand and signal for them to stand down.

The woman looks right at me as she takes a bite from the diseased, infested flesh. The bugs wiggle around the outside of her mouth while a tar-like substance slides through her teeth. She disappears into the night, and I'm not sure why I let her eat the fruit.

I pull the ultrasound photo from my pocket. It's like a storyboard panel, and I see a speck on the edge of the photo. Something faint. A little squiggle that might be a plant-hero-guy. And he's rushing from the edge of my periphery, charging the perimeter and scaling the fence to kill me and take the baby, to save this new child from a lifetime of villains.

Acknowledgements

I'm deeply grateful to Tim Z. Hernandez for feedback on early drafts of *Fruit Rot* and Ren Powell for feedback on later drafts. Additional thanks to Etchings Press for continually believing in my work. Lastly, thanks to you for reading and supporting small press literature.

About Etchings Press

Etchings Press is a student-run publisher at the University of Indianapolis that runs a post-publication award—the Whirling Prize—as well as an annual publication contest for one poetry chapbook, one prose chapbook, and one novella. On occasion, Etchings Press publishes new chapbooks from previous winners. The press is the new home for the Floodgate Poetry Series. For more information about these contests, the Whirling Prize post-publication award, and the Floodgate Poetry Series, please visit etchings.uindy.edu.

Previous winners and publications:

Poetry
2020: *Vaginas Need Air* by Tori Grant Welhouse
2019: *As Lovers Always Do* by Marne Wilson
2018: *In the Herald of Improbable Misfortunes*
    by Robert Campbell
2017: *Uncle Harold's Maxwell House Haggadah*
    by Danny Caine
2016: *Some Animals* by Kelli Allen
2015: *Velocity of Slugs* by Joey Connelly
2014: *Action at a Distance*
    by Christopher Petruccelli

Prose

2020: *Three in the Morning and You Don't Smoke Anymore*
   by Peter J. Stavros (fiction)
2019: *Dissenting Opinion from the Committee for the*
   Beatitudes by Marc J. Sheehan (fiction)
2018: *The Forsaken* by Chad V. Broughman (fiction)
2017: *Unravelings* by Sarah Cheshire (memoir)
2016: *Pathetic* by Shannon McLeod (essays)
2015: *Ologies* by Chelsea Biondolillo (essays)
2014: *Static: Stories* by Frederick Pelzer (fiction)

Novella

2020: *Under Black Leaves* by Doug Ramspeck
2019: *Savonne, Not Vonny* by Robin Lee Lovelace
2018: *Edge of the Known Bus Line* by James R. Gapinski
2017: *The Denialist's Almanac of American Plague*
   and Pestilence by Christopher Mohar
2016: *Followers* by Adam Fleming Petty

Chapbooks from Previous Winners

2020: *Fruit Rot* by James R. Gapinski (fiction)
2016: *#LOVESONG* by Chelsea Biondolillo
   (microessays with photos and found text)

James R. Gapinski is the author of *Edge of the Known Bus Line*—winner of the 2018 Etchings Press novella contest, named to *Kirkus Reviews'* Best Books of 2018, and a finalist for the 2019 Montaigne Medal. He is also the author of the flash collection *Messiah Tortoise*, available from Red Bird Chapbooks. James teaches for Southern New Hampshire University's MFA program, and he's managing editor of *The Conium Review*. Originally from southeastern Wisconsin, he now lives with his partner in Portland, Oregon.

Made in the USA
Middletown, DE
24 November 2020